Barb the Bird of Hope

written and illustrated
by
Zowie Norris

AuthorHouse™ UK
1663 Liberty Drive
Bloomington, IN 47403 USA
www.authorhouse.co.uk
UK TFN: 0800 0148641 (Toll Free inside the UK)
UK Local: 02036 956322 (+44 20 3695 6322 from outside the UK)

Because of the dynamic nature of the Internet, any web addresses or links contained in this book may have changed since publication and may no longer be valid. The views expressed in this work are solely those of the author and do not necessarily reflect the views of the publisher, and the publisher hereby disclaims any responsibility for them.

Any people depicted in stock imagery provided by Getty Images are models, and such images are being used for illustrative purposes only. Certain stock imagery © Getty Images.

This book is printed on acid-free paper.

ISBN: 978-1-6655-9031-0 (sc)
ISBN: 978-1-6655-9030-3 (e)

Print information available on the last page.

Published by AuthorHouse 06/15/2021

authorHOUSE·

Dedicated to Phoebe and Jasmine

In the centre of Bretton Park stood a tall and brightly blossomed laburnum tree. Apart from being an exquisite and attractive tree to admire, this tree was also the home of a rather unusual and exotic bird. It was a perfect home for this extremely pretty bird. The delicate blossoms that hung from the tree camouflaged her bright-yellow feathers exactly. The only different colour detected was her vivid violet tail feathers which spread out, fanning the sky on flight.

The tail feathers carefully twisted around the trunk of the tree in the evenings, but if you looked carefully, you would be able to spot her beady, glasslike eyes glistening between the dainty flowers. This bird was a well-known feature of Bretton Park, and many visited and admired her for different reasons. If you were lucky enough to see her full form in flight, she was truly a remarkable sight to see!

You might have correctly guessed that a bird such as this one did not always live at Bretton Park. She used to belong to the late Mr Davis, the Park House owner, who had named the bird after his youngest daughter, Barbara, because just like her, she was 'unique and mysterious'.

Back then, the bird, whom he called Barb, lived in a large iron birdcage that hung in the Park House kitchen. Mr Davis had underestimated just how large Barb would grow – especially her tail feathers. Although he enjoyed her company, he always felt sad that she did not get the chance to fly and explore as the other birds in the park did. Therefore, one day, he decided to set her free from her cage.

'Go and play and explore the park with the other birds. Be free! Stretch out your stunning wings wide, and spread your sunshine to others too, my beautiful Barb. I will never forget the joy you have brought to me,' cried Mr Davis. He wiped a tear from his eye as she soared gracefully out of the kitchen window that morning.

Swooping high into the clouds, Barb felt elated as she glided gracefully in the vast space around her. The sun was shining, and its golden rays made the park look even more inviting to her. Barb looped through the air with wild excitement above the lush green park. For many years, she had stared at the world through the kitchen window, hoping and longing to be able to explore it. Now her dreams had come true!

Barb perched on the top of an old oak tree, stopping to take in the view of the park before her. She saw the vast array of colourful flower beds; the different types of trees; the small birds with mainly brown, black and speckled feathers, flying between the trees; the children laughing and playing on the swings; the people strolling along the paths; and the old stone Park House.

Suddenly Barb felt sad. She loved Mr Davis and his family and had been a huge part of their lives for many years; she would miss them dearly. It was at that moment Barb decided to live in the park. This way, she could still see her human family each day too.

Barb soon made friends with the other birds in the park. Her striking and original appearance, about which she was never boastful, intrigued many of them. Even her sparrow friend James, who was known for being one of the grumpiest birds in the park, was keen to befriend Barb. She was a cheerful bird who loved her new sense of freedom and her ability to fly and sing with the other birds. Her care and attention towards them also helped the other birds to feel special and important too.

Although the majority of the park's birds were friendly, she soon found out that some of the cats, dogs and larger visiting birds were not as amenable. Evenings in the park brought out other menacing creatures too, and they easily spotted Barb, who was so unlike the other birds. In springtime when trees blossomed, the laburnum tree was the safest place for Barb to take her evening shelter in.

Being different in appearance never bothered Barb, despite the challenges that came with it, because she felt at home in the park, and the other birds accepted and welcomed her warmly.

During stormy days, when the sky was grey and dull, the grass was no longer lush or green but sludgy from the rain, and all the birds and animals hid or hibernated under the shelter of the tangled trees, Barb would suddenly fly out into the sky, her yellow feathers lighting up the dark day.

The sight of her golden silhouette and gleaming plumage against the grey sky, cheered up the other birds. To them she symbolised the hope for the return of brighter days in the park.

Barb did not symbolise hope just to the birds in the park either. As the time passed, she became familiar and started to feel safe and confident around some of the regular visitors to the park too.

Mr Ford had been visiting the gardens each morning since his beloved wife had sadly passed away. It had been their favourite place to go together – they loved the gardens especially. Barb had noticed how he always appeared to talk to the clouds as he sat on their favourite bench near the laburnum tree.

In truth, Mr Ford was speaking to his wife, and each day he searched the sky for some sort of sign that she was listening.

One morning, during Mr Ford's conversation with his wife, Barb began whistling a sweet tune in response. When he finally saw the beautiful bird at the top of the laburnum tree, he shook his head and laughed aloud.

''Are you OK?' asked Albert, the gardener, who was pruning the roses in the flowerbed nearby.

'Oh – yes. I thought the bird singing was something else', said Mr Ford, sniffing.

'Ah, that'll be Barb. She brightens up everyone's morning', laughed the gardener.

'She certainly does', replied Mr Ford smiling up at the tree. 'It was my wife's name too … that is my sign too.' He whispered the last bit up to the clouds.

Mr Ford continued to visit and speak to Barb each day, and he brought with him a bag of breadcrumbs as a treat for the bird.

Another daily park visitor also mirrored Mr Ford's kindness and generosity towards Barb. Dr Caverleri, who worked at the hospital next to the park, often had a quick lunch break on the bench near the laburnum tree. When he spotted Barb, his serious expression would transform into a broad smile, and his eyes would twinkle when he heard her beautiful song. The doctor enjoyed sharing his healthy lunch of nuts, seeds and fruits with her each day, whilst whistling a tune back to her in response to her song. The bird enjoyed his company too and trusted him enough, that one day she flew down from the top of the tree to perch on the arm of the bench beside him.

This small pocket of Dr Caverleri's time made him relax, see the beauty of life, reflect and clear his mind, leaving him ready to return to the ongoing challenges of his job. He had very important life-changing decisions to make each day, so this time was crucial to him – and to all of his patients too.

Gradually, Barb became more confident and began to make more appearances in the park, due to the love and kindness she received from the park visitors each day.

She no longer hid away behind the yellow tree blossoms and could now be often seen dancing in the air, gliding and twirling like a professional ice skater, with grace and elegance.

Barb began visiting other parts of the park now too – even the noisier parts, such as the play areas. The sounds of laughter and excitement from the children when they saw her made her feel proud and loved.

Word soon spread amongst the children that Bretton Park was the place where everyone hoped to see a special bird called Barb.

Many of the other birds in the park had never dared to go this close to the people who visited. They saw humans as dangerous animals and a threat to their existence. James the sparrow tried warning Barb not to get too near to them several times.

However, the kindness, compassion and generosity she received from people such as Mr Ford and Dr Caverleri, who talked to her, whistled and brought treats, and the smiles and laughter from the children in the park each day, refuted these opinions.

James told her of tales about bad people who had littered the park, resulting in some of the animals being poorly. However, Barb reminded him how Albert, the park gardener, spent each day tending to the trees and plants in the park and how the park rangers worked with groups of school children to clean up the park too.

Her positive view of humans started to give some of the other birds more hope that they could trust people too, and a few started to join Barb when she received her daily visits, moving close to enjoy the occasional treats people brought.

Sadly, the birds' happy life in the park suddenly changed one day. The park became silent and still. No visitors came to the park at all that day. No treats appeared. No laughter sounded. Even Albert did not come to water the plants. Everything seemed to stop.

Barb flew around the entire park looking for some sign of human beings but saw nothing.

'This is what I was trying to warn you about, Barb', tweeted James. 'People don't really care about us – they've probably got bored and moved to a different park.'

'No – something isn't right', replied Barb. She refused to believe what James was saying was true. She perched on the main entrance gate, waiting patiently for her human friends. Barb did notice that some kind of new sign that was attached to the gate today.

'Where is everyone?' she wondered.

The following day was the same. Silence.

'Did anyone see Albert this morning?' Barb asked the other birds.

'No. That gate has not opened to anyone yet. I'm starting to wonder if James was right', replied Tristan the blackbird.

'Not you too! Well, I'm not giving up hope yet. I'm off to find out what is actually going on', replied Barb. 'People who visit each day don't just stop coming. There has to be something amiss, and I need to investigate this out of the park today and quickly'.

So off she flew.

It had been a while since Barb had left the park. She had never liked how noisy, busy and crowded the town appeared to be; the people there always seemed to be in a rush or too occupied to spend any time with her.

Today it was extremely different.

The streets were empty and quiet, as though time stood still.

That's odd! thought Barb.

There was not a single person around and no cars driving down the street. The shops appeared to be closed too.

Barb flew anxiously down the main street to return to the park, but suddenly the ear-piercing siren of an ambulance speeding towards Bretton Hospital interrupted the silence.

Barb jolted from the noise and then thought, *The people haven't totally vanished after all!*

As she flew towards the hospital, she noticed there appeared to be a frenzy of movement between the vehicles, with doctors, nurses and patients arriving.

All of them appeared to be wearing masks that covered their faces too – even the people arriving at the hospital.

I wonder why so many people need to go to the hospital today. No wonder Dr Caverleri has not had time to visit me! thought Barb as she returned to the park and the comfort of her laburnum tree.

The following day, Barb decided to fly to the Park House and visit Mrs Davis; she had not seen her for a while. She perched on the window ledge of the kitchen and whistled her greeting call.

Mrs Davis, however, was engaged with something on her television. It sounded very serious.

Barb flew up to the bedroom window ledge to see the girls. Phoebe and Jasmine were busy playing a game on their computer. The window was open this time, so Jasmine heard her tune.

'Oh, it's Barb … hi', said Jasmine, coming to the window. 'I wish that I could come outside and play with you, but the prime minister has told everyone to isolate because of the virus.' She sighed.

'Barb doesn't understand that! Are you playing this game or what?' called Phoebe.

'Coming! Bye, Barb', said Jasmine, returning to the computer.

Virus? Isolation? thought Barb as she returned to her tree. *What are these new words? Whatever they are, perhaps they are the reason why people have stopped coming to the park and cannot leave their homes.*

When Barb had lived in the cage in the kitchen, she had felt protected but trapped.

Perhaps this is how the people feel too, she thought. *Will this situation last forever? How can things get better?*

That night, though, things took a turn for the worse. A huge storm shook the park. Lightning crackled and streaked across the sky, followed by the loud crash and rumble of thunder. Strong winds and torrential rain rattled the laburnum tree aggressively; the delicate yellow blossoms on the tree were scattered like a yellow snow shower. It was too dangerous to stay in the shaking and breaking tree, so Barb took shelter in the roof of the park bandstand, which appeared to be the only sturdy and still form amidst the raging weather.

The storm lasted for many hours. Barb had managed to curl into a small corner of the roof, huddling up with some of her other bird friends who had had the same idea as she did.

'I am so s … s … scared, Barb', stuttered one of the young pigeons called Penny.

'Me too!' chirped her brothers George and Bobby in unison.

'We are all doomed!' cried James the sparrow from the other corner of the roof.

'Be brave, James! Well, at least the plants will have had a good water in Albert's absence', Barb replied, trying to cheer the pigeons up and prevent them from being frightened. She could always see the positive side of things, no matter what the situation.

When the rain died down and the winds finally stopped, Barb decided to leave her shelter. The picture of chaos and destruction in front of her was devastating. Her beautiful park was in tatters. Fence panels were broken and missing, many trees had snapped branches which were strewn all over, plants were a tangled mess, and the colourful flowerbeds – Albert's pride – had missing flower heads and ripped petals scattered all over the grass like used confetti.

Worst of all, Barb's beautiful laburnum tree home was destroyed. Lightning had hit the main branch, splitting the tree down the centre.

Feeling scared and sorrowful, Barb flew away from the park for the second time.

What next! Everything I love is being taken away from me, thought Barb as she flew. She had never felt the need to leave the park until now, but everything felt so hopeless, and her first instinct was to fly away, as if it never happened. She thought about her bird friends, who might also have lost their homes, and how upset they would be too – and now she was not there to help or reassure them. She decided to stop for a rest and reflect on the situation further, perching on the window ledge of one of the high windows on Bretton Hospital.

Through the window, she could see an elderly woman lying in a bed. A young nurse entered the room wearing a face mask.

'I know that you are worried about your positive Covid test, Joan, but your temperature has come down, and now you have your appetite back too. These are good signs that you are on the road to recovery', said the nurse reassuringly. Although you could not see her face fully, she had kind and smiling eyes, and her words appeared to comfort Joan.

What a kind and caring young lady, thought Barb, and she hopped to the next window ledge.

Through this window, Barb could see an elderly man chatting with a young woman in a mask at his bedside. She was quietly sobbing.

'Don't get upset, Kelly. I am in the best place, and you mustn't give up hope. I will fight this virus with the help of these amazing doctors and nurses. I know they are working on new vaccines already', said the man, patting her hand.

What a brave man, thought Barb, and she hopped to the next window ledge.

In the next room, she saw a young nurse removing some plastic gloves and washing his hands whilst talking to another nurse, who was collecting her coat from a locker. He looked weary and emotional.

'What a day! It seems to be affecting many', he said, sighing.

'I know – they didn't prepare us for a pandemic at college!' replied his colleague.

'I'd better try to get some sleep. I'm back in six hours – they are short staffed, so I've offered to help out.'

'You are an angel. See you in a bit; make sure you get some rest', responded the nurse as she left the room.

No wonder that man had so much hope with nurses like these, thought Barb, and she hopped to the next window ledge.

Barb recognised the twinkly eyes belonging to the doctor in the next room – Dr Caverleri! He was working at his computer. He looked tired but pleased with himself.

His eyes wandered above the screen, and his smile instantly widened as he caught sight of his favourite feathered friend.

'Why, if it isn't Barb! Have you come to visit me this time?' he said. He scooped a few seeds from his lunch box and brought them to the window. 'I'm sorry that I haven't been to visit you; things have been really busy recently. But today I have some hope with a new vaccine that has been created.'

Dr Caverleri opened the window and held out his hand flat, with a few pumpkin seeds in the centre of his palm. Barb gratefully accepted the treat, allowing him to stroke her wings with his free hand. She felt happy once more.

'Now fly, my beautiful bird of hope, and sing your beautiful song to the world. We will beat this virus!' cried the doctor.

Barb took flight once again, and she thought about what she had seen in the hospital. No matter what hardship and challenges these people were facing, they remained kind, caring and brave, never giving up hope. She decided to return home to the park; there was no place that she would rather be.

As the rays of the sun burst through the clouds, a shimmering rainbow appeared over the park.

Now I know why Mr Ford talks to the clouds, thought Barb. *That's my sign too. I know now that one day everything will be OK, and I will hear the laughter of children in the park once again. Just as I was freed from my cage, the people will be free from their homes again.*

As she entered the park, she heard a familiar voice calling her name.

'Oh, Barb, it's so good to see you! You are OK – thank goodness! When I saw that the storm had damaged your tree, I feared the worst!' cried Albert.

He had been busy tidying up the park, and it was starting to look so much better for it too.

Another familiar voice also called her name. It appeared that Mr Ford had been helping Albert to tidy up the park and was busy digging near the bench where he sat each day. He cried out with joy when he saw his beloved bird perched on the handle of Albert's spade.

When he stepped to the side, to Barb's delight, she saw the familiar beautiful yellow blossoms of a new laburnum tree.

'Hope you like your new home', he said with pride. 'Now you can continue to bring hope to everyone who visits the park when it opens again.'

'The park wouldn't be the same without you. Welcome home!' chirped James the sparrow from a nearby bush.

About the Author

 Zowie Norris is delighted to share her first published story. She graduated with an English and teaching degree at Bretton Hall College, West Yorkshire, England in 1998. Until this point, she has shared her passion for creative writing with her two daughters, Phoebe and Jasmine, and for the past 17 years as a primary teacher and 6 years as a Headteacher in Yorkshire. Her aim was always to publish her work for other children to enjoy too.

Although the story is fictional, Barb the Bird of Hope is named after her mother who sadly passed away five years ago.

Zowie had a happy childhood, a close family who encouraged her creativity and has many positive memories which she is aims to replicate with her husband and daughters. The loss of her beloved mother and the anxieties around the pandemic have highlighted the importance of family, gratitude and helping others to have hope too, inspiring her to write this story.